This book belongs to

DIANE GOODE'S
✶ AMERICAN ✶
CHRISTMAS

SCHOLASTIC INC. · NEW YORK TORONTO LONDON AUCKLAND SYDNEY

The publisher gratefully acknowledges permission to reprint on:

page 8, "December" by Aileen Fisher, reproduced by permission of the author from *That's Why*. New York: Nelson, 1946. Copyright renewed.

page 16, "Carol of the Brown King," reprinted by permission of Harold Ober Associates Incorporated. Copyright © 1958 by Langston Hughes. Copyright renewed 1986 by George Houston Bass.

pages 22–27, "Mr. Willowby's Christmas Tree" by Robert Barry. New York: McGraw-Hill, 1963. Reproduced by permission of the publisher.

pages 28–29, "I'll Be Home for Christmas." Words: Kim Gannon. Music: Walter Kent. © Gannon & Kent Music, 1943. Renewed.

pages 31–37, "The Puppy Who Wanted a Boy," copyright © 1958 by Jane Thayer. By permission of Morrow Junior Books (a division of William Morrow and Company, Inc.).

pages 51–56, "Christmas on the Banks of Plum Creek," excerpt from *On the Banks of Plum Creek*, by Laura Ingalls Wilder. Text copyright © 1937 by Laura Ingalls Wilder, renewed 1965 by Roger L. MacBride. Reprinted by permission of Harper & Row, Publishers, Inc.

pages 58–59, "little tree" is reprinted from *Tulips & Chimneys* by E. E. Cummings, edited by George James Firmage, by permission of Liveright Publishing Corporation. Copyright 1923, 1925 and renewed 1951, 1953 by E. E. Cummings. Copyright © 1973, 1976 by the Trustees for the E. E. Cummings Trust. Copyright © 1973, 1976 by George James Firmage.

page 66, "Merry Christmas," from *Feathered Ones and Furry* by Aileen Fisher. (Thomas Y. Crowell.) Copyright © 1971 by Aileen Fisher. Reprinted by permission of Harper & Row, Publishers, Inc.

page 67, "Christmas Eve Rhyme," from *Sweet as a Pickle and Clean as a Pig* by Carson McCullers. Copyright © 1964 by Carson McCullers and Rolf Gerard. Reprinted by permission of Houghton Mifflin Company.

pages 68–69, "Silver Bells," by Jay Livingston & Ray Evans. Copyright © 1950 by Paramount Music Corporation. Copyright renewed 1977 Paramount Music Corporation, 1 Gulf & Western Plaza, New York, NY 10023. International copyright secured. Made in USA. All rights reserved. Used by permission.

pages 71–80, "The Night Before Christmas" by Thyra Turner, reprinted by permission of Charles Scribner's Sons, an imprint of Macmillan Publishing Company, from *Christmas House* by Thyra Turner. Copyright 1943 Charles Scribner's Sons; copyright renewed © 1971.

ISBN 0-590-45446-3

This collection copyright © 1990 by Dutton Children's Books. Illustrations copyright © 1990 by Diane Goode. All rights reserved. Published by Scholastic Inc., 730 Broadway, New York, NY 10003, by arrangement with Dutton Children's Books, a division of Penguin Books USA Inc.

12 11 10 9 8 7 6 5 4 3 2   2 3 4 5 6 7/9

Printed in the U.S.A.   08

First Scholastic printing, November 1992

FOR PETER

CONTENTS

INTRODUCTION

The very word *Christmas* is enough to bring gleeful smiles and shivers of anticipation to a child—and to anyone who ever was one. No holiday has more appeal. We Americans give our own distinct expression to this holiday celebrated around the world. And because our country is one of such diversity and breadth, there are as many ways to celebrate as there are groups that came to this country bringing their own traditions. In this land of immigrants, we have maintained some customs, adopted others, created still others, and, in the mixing, made them our own. Like a crazy quilt, the American Christmas celebration is a lovingly made collection to be passed on to the next generation.

Christmas has many meanings, but I think of this festive holiday as a time for celebrating our children and for dusting off the childlike delight we keep in our own hearts. It's a time for family togetherness, for sharing and caring and giving, for keeping alive old traditions and starting new ones.

In our home, we trim the tree with decorations collected over the years. What a thrill it is when the lights go on! My son and I

bake gingerbread men and distribute them to our friends, then come home to a candlelight dinner of roast goose. Before bed, we read *A Visit from St. Nicholas,* which is as magical to me now as it was when I first heard it. Then we listen carefully for the sound of tiny hooves. We always hear them.

In this book, I have tried to find stories, poems, and songs that families will enjoy reading aloud and singing together during the Christmas season. Some are funny; some touch our hearts. The selections come from different periods in our country's short history, and originated in different parts of the country and from various ethnic groups. The authors of some stories and poems are among the most illustrious in American literature. Other selections spring from our rich oral folk heritage. Some of the pieces should be as comfortably familiar and loved as the smell of pine needles and spicy cookies. Others, I hope, are new to you. Like presents piled under the tree, there are many to choose from. Surely you will find at least one among them to love. I hope this book will become part of your family's Christmas tradition.

DECEMBER

Aileen Fisher

I like days
with a snow-white collar,
and nights when the moon
is a silver dollar,
and hills are filled
with eiderdown stuffing
and your breath makes smoke
like an engine puffing.

I like days
when feathers are snowing,
and all the eaves
have petticoats showing,
and the air is cold,
and the wires are humming,
but you feel all warm ...
with Christmas coming!

9

THE PETERKINS'
CHRISTMAS TREE
Lucretia Peabody Hale

Early in the autumn the Peterkins began to prepare for their Christmas tree. Mr. Peterkin had been up to Mr. Bromwick's wood lot and selected the tree, and at length had it cut down and brought secretly into the barn. A week or two before Christmas a measurement was made of it. To Mr. Peterkin's great dismay it was discovered that it was too high to stand in the back parlor.

Agamemnon suggested that it might be set up slanting; but Mrs. Peterkin was very sure it would make her dizzy, and the candles would drip.

But a brilliant idea came to Mr. Peterkin. He proposed that the ceiling of the parlor should be raised to make room for the top of the tree.

Elizabeth Eliza objected to having the whole ceiling raised, because her room was over the back parlor, and she would have no floor while the alteration was going on. Besides, if the floor were raised, perhaps she could not walk in her room upright.

Mr. Peterkin explained that he didn't propose altering the whole ceiling, but to lift up a ridge across the room at the back part where the tree was to stand. This would make a hump in Elizabeth Eliza's room. Elizabeth Eliza said she would not mind that.

On consulting the carpenter, however, he insisted that the tree could be cut off at the lower end to suit the height of the parlor and demurred at so great a change as altering the ceiling. But Mr. Peterkin had set his mind upon the improvement.

So the folding doors into the back parlor were closed, and for nearly a fortnight before Christmas there was great litter of fallen plastering, and laths, and chips, and shavings.

All this delighted the little boys. They could not understand what was going on. Perhaps they suspected a Christmas tree, but they did not know why a Christmas tree should have so many chips, and were still more astonished at the hump that appeared in Elizabeth Eliza's room. It must be a Christmas present, or else the tree in a box.

Elizabeth Eliza meanwhile was pretty busy in her own room; the furniture had to be changed, and the carpet altered. The "hump" was higher than Elizabeth Eliza expected. There was danger of bumping her own head whenever she crossed it. She had to nail some padding on the ceiling for fear of accidents.

The afternoon before Christmas, Elizabeth Eliza, Solomon John, and their father collected in the back parlor for a council. The carpenters had done their work, and the tree stood at its full height at the back of the room, the top stretching up into the space arranged for it. All the chips and shavings were cleared away, and it stood on a neat box.

But what were they to put upon the tree? After all her trips into town Elizabeth Eliza had forgotten to bring anything for it. "I thought of candies and sugarplums," she said; "but I concluded if we made caramels ourselves we should not need them. But, then, we have not made caramels."

A gloom came over the room. Solomon John proposed going into town. He lighted a match to examine the newspaper about the trains. There were plenty of trains coming out at that hour, but none going in except a very late one. That would not leave time to do anything and come back.

At this moment there was a loud knocking at the front door. The door was opened, and there was a man, pulling in a large box.

The box was addressed to Elizabeth Eliza. It was from the lady from Philadelphia! The box was opened directly. There was every kind of gilt hanging-thing, from gilt peapods to butterflies on springs. There were shining flags and lanterns, and birdcages, and nests with birds sitting on them, baskets of fruit, gilt apples and bunches of grapes, and, at the bottom of the whole, a large box of candles and a box of Philadelphia bonbons!

Elizabeth Eliza and Solomon John could scarcely keep from screaming.

Hastily Mr. Peterkin and the rest took out the things and hung them on the tree, and put on the candles.

When all was done, it looked so well that Mr. Peterkin exclaimed:

"Let us light the candles now, and send to invite all the neighbors tonight, and have the tree on Christmas Eve!"

And so it was that the Peterkins had their Christmas tree the day before, and on Christmas night could go and visit their neighbors.

CAROL
OF THE BROWN KING
Langston Hughes

Of the three Wise Men
Who came to the King,
One was a brown man,
So they sing.

Of the three Wise Men
Who followed the Star,
One was a brown king
From afar.

They brought fine gifts
Of spices and gold
In jeweled boxes
Of beauty untold.

Unto His humble
Manger they came
And bowed their heads
In Jesus' name.

Three Wise Men,
One dark like me—
Part of His
Nativity.

JINGLE BELLS

John Pierpont

VERSE

Dash - ing through the snow, in a one - horse o - pen sleigh,

o'er the fields we go, laugh - ing all the way.

Bells on bob - tail ring, mak - ing spir - its bright. What

fun it is to ride and sing a sleigh - ing song to - night!

CHORUS

Jin - gle bells, jin - gle bells, jin - gle all the way.

Oh, what fun it is to ride in a one-horse o - pen sleigh. ___

Jin - gle bells, jin - gle bells, jin - gle all the way.

Oh, what fun it is to ride in a one-horse o - pen sleigh!

YES, VIRGINIA,
THERE IS A SANTA CLAUS

In 1897, a little girl in New York City wrote a letter to the *New York Sun*.

Dear Editor:

I am eight years old. Some of my little friends say that there is no Santa Claus. Papa says, "If you see it in the *Sun*, it's so." Please tell me the truth. Is there a Santa Claus?

Virginia O'Hanlon

The editor Francis P. Church answered in the following editorial:

IS THERE A SANTA CLAUS?

Virginia, your little friends are wrong. They have been affected by the skepticism of a skeptical age. They think that nothing can be which is not comprehensible by their little minds. They do not believe except what they see.

Yes, Virginia, there is a Santa Claus. He exists as certainly as love and generosity and devotion exist. Alas, how dreary the world would be if there were no Santa Claus! It would be as dreary as if there were no Virginias! There would be no childlike faith, then, no poetry, no romance, to make tolerable this existence.

You might get your papa to hire men to watch all the chimneys on Christmas Eve to catch Santa Claus; but even if they did not see Santa Claus coming down, what would that prove? Not everybody sees Santa Claus. The most real things in the world are those that neither children nor men see.

No Santa Claus! Thank God, he lives, and he lives forever. A thousand years from now, Virginia, nay, ten times ten thousand years from now, he will continue to make glad the heart of childhood.

MR. WILLOWBY'S CHRISTMAS TREE

Robert Barry

Mr. Willowby's Christmas tree
Came by special delivery.
Full and fresh and glistening green—
The biggest tree he had ever seen.
He dashed downstairs
   to open the door—
This was the moment
   he'd waited for.
"A magnificent tree! Splendid!"
   he cried.
"Please, sir, won't you carry it
   right inside.
I think it might look best this year
Right in the parlor corner here."
But once the tree stood in its place,
Mr. Willowby made a terrible face.
The tree touched the ceiling, then bent like a bow.
"Oh good heavens," he gasped. "Something must go!"

Baxter, the butler, was called on in haste,
To chop off the top, though it seemed quite a waste.
"That's great,"
    Mr. Willowby cried with glee;
"Now we can start
    to trim my tree."
When the trimming
    was well under way,
The top was placed
    on a silver tray.
Baxter said,
    "I know just who'd be
Delighted
    with this Christmas tree."

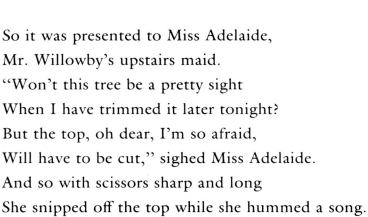

So it was presented to Miss Adelaide,
Mr. Willowby's upstairs maid.
"Won't this tree be a pretty sight
When I have trimmed it later tonight?
But the top, oh dear, I'm so afraid,
Will have to be cut," sighed Miss Adelaide.
And so with scissors sharp and long
She snipped off the top while she hummed a song.

The top was set out the very next day
In back of the house to be thrown away.
That little treetop caught the eye
Of Tim, the gardener, passing by.
He certainly was not about
To see that little tree thrown out.
"Fa la la . . . Surprise! Surprise!"
His wife could not believe her eyes.
"But our house," she said,
    "is so snug and small
I do not believe we need it all!"
And before Tim had a chance to shout
She cut off the top and threw it out.

Barnaby Bear was padding by—
It almost hit him in the eye.
"Now who would throw a tree away
So very close to Christmas Day?
I'll take it home, that's what I'll do!
Look, Mama Bear, I've a present for you."

"Isn't it a pretty tree,"
Yawned Mama Bear quite drowsily.
"Before we go to sleep this year
Let's have a Christmas party, dear."
But Little Bear, standing off far,
Cried out, "That tree won't hold a star!"
Barnaby said, "Let's cut a hunk
Off at the bottom, here at the trunk."
But Mama Bear just shook her head,
And sliced the treetop off instead.

"Jolly, by golly!" Barnaby said with a kick.
"Mama, that surely is just the right trick.
Let's trim it with bells and honey rings,
Some berries, and tinsel, and popcorn on strings."
Mama said, "Trim it just as you like,
I've got to tidy up for the night.
This top we won't need any more;
I'll put it just outside the door."

Later on that frosty night,
Frisky Fox came into sight.
He spied the treetop, rubbed his chin,
Opened his sack and stuffed the top in.
He scampered home and jumped his gate—
This Christmas present couldn't wait.
"It's even better than mincemeat pie,"
Said Mrs. Fox with a happy sigh.
Then the Foxes saw
    that their Christmas prize
Was just a wee bit oversize.
"There, my dears, now don't you worry.
I'll fix this top now in a hurry."

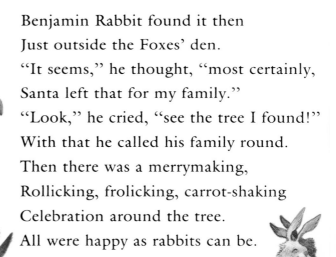

Benjamin Rabbit found it then
Just outside the Foxes' den.
"It seems," he thought, "most certainly,
Santa left that for my family."
"Look," he cried, "see the tree I found!"
With that he called his family round.
Then there was a merrymaking,
Rollicking, frolicking, carrot-shaking
Celebration around the tree.
All were happy as rabbits can be.

Benjamin Rabbit, with his own hand,
Sliced a carrot and made a stand.
"Now let's see how this will look
In our little chimney nook."
But right away, the children cried,
"Look, it's leaning off to one side!"
"It's too tall, that's all," said Mrs. Rabbit,
And as though it were a summer carrot,
She gave it a chop
And threw away ... the top!

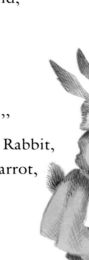

Then Mistletoe Mouse just happened to see
That tiny top of a Christmas tree.
He pulled it through the snow and ice ...
Up some stairs ...
He fell down twice!

At last he reached his cozy house.
"It's just the right size!" said Mrs. Mouse.
Then at the top, if you please,
They put a star made out of cheese.
Oh, wasn't it grand to have a tree—
Exactly like Mr. Willowby?

I'LL BE HOME FOR CHRISTMAS

Kim Gannon and Walter Kent

I'll be home for Christ-mas;___ you can plan on me.___

Please have snow and mis-tle-toe and pre-sents on the tree.___

Christ-mas Eve will find me___ where the love-light gleams.___

I'll be home for Christ-mas, if on-ly in my dreams.___

THE PUPPY
WHO WANTED A BOY

Jane Thayer

One day Petey, who was a puppy, said to his mother, "I'd like a boy for Christmas."

His mother, who was a dog, said she guessed he could have a boy if he was a very good puppy.

So the day before Christmas, Petey's mother asked, "Have you been a very good puppy?"

"Oh yes!" said Petey.

"I guess you've been good," said his mother. "Anyway, you're awfully little. I shall go out and get you a boy for Christmas."

But when Petey's mother came back, she looked very much worried.

"How would you like a soft, white rabbit with pink ears for Christmas?" she said to Petey.

"No thanks," said Petey.

"Don't you want a lovely canary?"

"No, I just wanted a boy."

"How about some guppy fish? They're nice," said Petey's mother.

"I don't like fish," said Petey. "I'd like a boy."

"Petey," said his mother, "there are no boys to be had."

"No boys?" exclaimed Petey in dismay.

"Not one could I find. They're terribly short of boys this year."

Petey felt as if he couldn't stand it if he didn't have a boy.

Finally his mother said, "There, now, there must be a boy somewhere. Perhaps you could find some dog who would be glad to give his boy away."

So Petey hopefully started off.

It wasn't long before he saw a collie racing with a boy on a bicycle. Petey trembled with joy.

He called out to the collie, "Excuse me. Do you want to give your boy away?"

But the collie said *no,* he definitely *didn't,* in a dreadful tone of voice.

Petey sat down. He watched the collie and his boy on a bicycle until they were out of his sight.

"I didn't really want a boy on a bicycle anyway," said Petey.

After a while, he saw a red setter playing ball with a boy. Petey was just delighted.

But he remembered how cross the collie had been. So he sat down on the sidewalk and called out politely, "Excuse me. Do you want to give your boy away?"

But the setter said *no,* he definitely *didn't,* in a terrifying tone of voice!

"Oh, well," said Petey, trotting off, "I don't think playing ball is much."

Soon Petey came to a bulldog, sitting in a car with a boy. Petey was pleased, for he was getting a little tired from so much walking.

So he called out loudly, but very politely, "Excuse me. Do you want to give your boy away?"

But the bulldog said *no,* he definitely *didn't,* and he growled in Petey's face.

"Oh, dear!" said Petey. He ran off behind a house and stayed there until the bulldog and his boy drove away.

"Well, who wants to go riding in a car? Pff! Not me!" said Petey.

After a while he met a Scotty, walking with his boy and carrying a package in his mouth.

"Now that is a good kind of boy!" said Petey. "If I had a boy to take walks with and carry packages for, there might be some dog biscuit or cookies in the package."

He stayed across the street and shouted at the top of his lungs, but polite as could be, "Excuse me. Do you want to give your boy away?"

The Scotty had his mouth full of package. But he managed to say *no,* he definitely *didn't,* and he showed his sharp teeth at Petey.

"I guess that wasn't the kind of boy I wanted either," said poor Petey. "But my goodness, where *will* I find a boy?"

Petey went on and on. He saw Irish terriers, Scotch terriers, Skye terriers. He saw foxhounds, greyhounds, wolfhounds. He saw pointers, setters, spaniels, beagles, chows.

He asked every dog politely. But he couldn't find a single dog who would give his boy away.

Petey's ears began to droop. His tail grew limp. His legs were *so* tired. "My mother was right," he thought. "There isn't a boy to be had."

As it was getting dark, he came to a large building on the very edge of town. Petey was going by, very slowly because his paws hurt, when he saw a sign over the door. The sign said:

ORPHANS' HOME

"I know what orphans are," Petey said to himself. "They're children who have no mother, and no dog to take care of them either. Maybe I could find a boy here!"

He padded slowly up the walk of the Orphans' Home. He was so tired he could hardly lift his paws.

Then Petey stopped. He listened. He could hear music. He looked. Through the window he could see a lighted Christmas tree, and children singing carols.

On the front step of the Orphans' Home, all by himself, sat a boy! He was not a very big boy. He looked lonely.

Petey gave a glad little cry. He forgot about being tired. He leaped up the walk and landed in the boy's lap.

Sniff, sniff went Petey's little nose. Wiggle, wag went Petey's tail. He licked the boy with his warm, wet tongue.

How glad the boy was to see Petey! He put both his arms around the little dog and hugged him tight.

Then the front door opened. "Goodness, Dickie," a lady said, "what are you doing out here? Come on in to the Christmas tree."

Petey sat very still.

The boy looked up at the lady. Then he looked down at Petey. Petey began to tremble. Would the boy go in and leave him?

But the boy said, "I've got a puppy. Can he come, too?"

"A puppy!" The lady came over and looked down at Petey. "Why," she said, "you're a nice dog. Wherever did you come from? Yes, bring him in."

"Come on, puppy," said the boy, and in they scampered.

A crowd of boys was playing around the Christmas tree. They all rushed at Petey. They all wanted to pick him up. They all wanted to pet him.

Petey wagged his tail. He wagged his fat little body. He frisked about and licked every boy who came near.

"Can he stay?" the boys asked.

"Yes," said the lady, "he may stay."

Petey wriggled away from the hands that petted him. Dickie was the one he loved best.

"But who ever would think," said Petey to himself, "that I'd get *fifty* boys for Christmas!"

WELCOME HERE!
Traditional Shaker Poem

Welcome here, welcome here,
All be alive and be of good cheer.

I've got a pie all baked complete,
Pudding too, that's very sweet.
Chestnuts are roasting, join us here
While we dance and make good cheer.

I've got a log that's burning hot,
Toddy's bubbling in the pot.
Come in, ye people, where it's warm,
The wind blows sharp and it may storm.

I made a loaf that's cooling there,
With my neighbors, I will share.
Come, all ye people, hear me sing
A song of friendly welcoming.

Welcome here, welcome here,
All be alive and be of good cheer.

AWAY IN A MANGER
Traditional American Carol

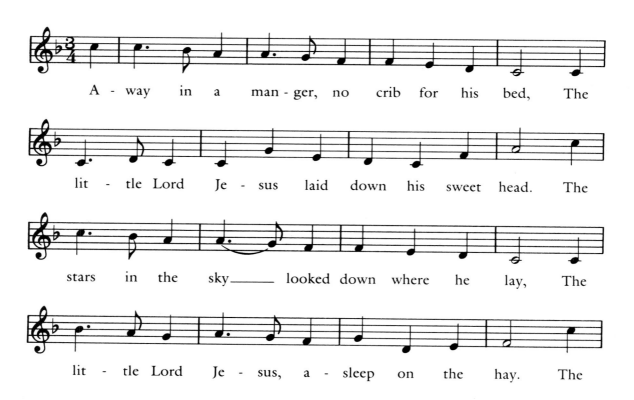

A - way in a man - ger, no crib for his bed, The

lit - tle Lord Je - sus laid down his sweet head. The

stars in the sky_____ looked down where he lay, The

lit - tle Lord Je - sus, a - sleep on the hay. The

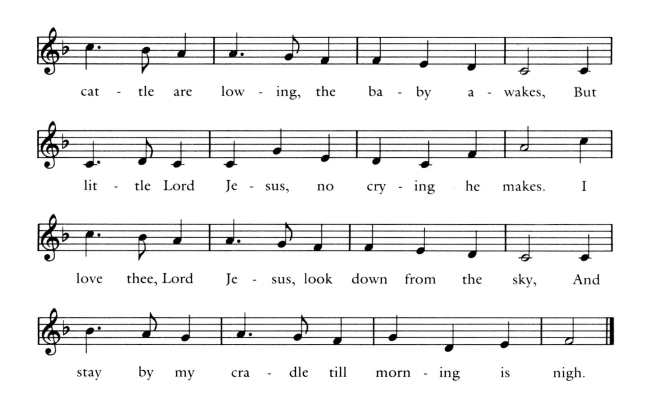

cat - tle are low - ing, the ba - by a - wakes, But

lit - tle Lord Je - sus, no cry - ing he makes. I

love thee, Lord Je - sus, look down from the sky, And

stay by my cra - dle till morn - ing is nigh.

41

A BAKER'S DOZEN

Folktale from Upstate New York

In the year 1655 on the last day of December, a baker, Baas, was working late in his shop in Albany. He was selling his St. Nicholas cookies that had carried his fame far down the Hudson River. He was about to shut up shop when an uncommonly ugly old woman thrust her way in, demanding a dozen of the special Christmas cookies.

Looking into the fragrant bag the baker handed her, she said crossly: "One more cookie, I said a dozen."

"You have a dozen," said Baas. "I carefully counted twelve of my finest cookies."

"One more cookie," demanded the old woman. "One more than twelve makes a dozen."

Baas grabbed her by the shoulder and pushed her to the door. "A dozen is a dozen. You may go to the Devil for another cookie!" he shouted. "You won't get it here."

Later, when he told this story to his wife, she suggested that on a holiday eve he should perhaps have given the woman an extra cookie. But Baas reminded her that business was business.

In the months that followed, mysterious bad luck came to Baas' little bakery. Money and cookies disappeared, as if snatched up by invisible hands. Bread rose to the ceiling or fell flat as a pancake. A handsome brick oven collapsed. The stubborn baker began to wonder whether supernatural powers were not at work.

A year passed this way. On the next New Year's Eve the memory of the old woman's appearance was so vivid that Baas exclaimed: "Holy Saint Nicholas, suppose that witch comes again! What shall I do?"

As the baker spoke these words, there appeared before him the good saint, smiling with holiday kindness. "Well, Baas," said St. Nicholas, "you were speaking my name so here I am. This whole trouble can be resolved if you have the spirit which my holidays demand."

The figure of the saint vanished. In its place stood the ugly old woman demanding a dozen cookies. Baas rapidly counted thirteen of them, presenting the bag to her with a bow and a "Happy New Year!"

"The spell is broken, Baas," said the witch. "Now swear to me on the likeness of Saint Nicholas that hereafter in Albany thirteen will make a baker's dozen."

Baas took the oath. And from that day to this, a baker's dozen means thirteen.

THE BELLS

Edgar Allan Poe

Hear the sledges with the bells—
    Silver bells!
What a world of merriment their melody
    foretells!
   How they tinkle, tinkle, tinkle,
    In the icy air of night!
   While the stars, that oversprinkle
   All the heavens, seem to twinkle
    With a crystalline delight
   Keeping time, time, time,
    In a sort of Runic rhyme,
To the tintinnabulation that so musically wells
   From the bells, bells, bells, bells,
    Bells, bells, bells—
From the jingling and the tinkling of the bells.

PIÑATA SONG

Traditional Mexican Song

Da - le, da - le, da - le, no pier - das el ti - no.
Hit it, hit it, hit it, swing it all a - round___.

Mi - de la dis - tan - cia que hay en el ca - mi - no.
Feel your way, go for - ward, bring it crash - ing down___.

No quiero oro   Don't want any gold, and
Ni quiero plata.   Don't want any silver.
Yo lo que quiero   Want to be the one who
Es romper la piñata.   Brings down the piñata.

49

CHRISTMAS ON THE BANKS OF PLUM CREEK

Laura Ingalls Wilder

That was another mild winter without much snow. But chill winds blew, the sky was grey, and the best place for little girls was in the cozy house.

Every morning Laura and Mary studied their books and worked sums on the slate. Every afternoon Ma heard their lessons.

Every Sunday they went to Sunday school. Laura saw Nellie Oleson showing off her fur cape, and she burned hot inside. She knew that hot feeling was wicked. She knew she must forgive Nellie, or she would never be an angel. She thought hard about the pictures of beautiful angels in the big paper-covered Bible at home. But they wore long white nightgowns. Not one of them wore a fur cape.

One afternoon Ma said there would be no lessons, because they must all get ready to go to town that night. Laura and Mary were astonished.

"But we never go to town at night!" Mary said.

"There must always be a first time," said Ma.

"But why must there be, Ma?" Laura asked. "Why are we going to town at night?"

"It's a surprise," said Ma. "Now, no more questions. We must all take baths, and be our very nicest."

Ma brought in the washtub and heated water for Mary's bath. Then again for Laura's bath, and again for Carrie's. There had never been such scrubbing and scampering, such a changing to fresh drawers and petticoats, such brushing of shoes and braiding of hair and tying on of hair ribbons. There had never been such a wondering.

The wagon box was full of clean hay. Pa put Mary and Laura in it and wrapped blankets around them. He climbed to the seat beside Ma and drove away toward town.

The stars were small and frosty in the dark sky. The horses' feet clippety-clopped and the wagon rattled over the hard ground.

The town seemed asleep. The stores were dark as Pa drove past them. Then Laura exclaimed, "Oh, look at the church! How pretty the church is!"

The church was full of light. Light spilled out of all its windows and ran out into the darkness from the door when it opened to let someone in.

Pa drove to the church steps and helped them all out. They waited in the cold until he had covered the horses with their blankets. Then he came, and they all went into the church together.

Laura's mouth fell open and her eyes stretched to look at what she saw. She held Mary's hand tightly and they followed Ma and Pa. They sat down. Then Laura could look with all her might.

Standing in front of the crowded benches was a tree. Laura

decided it must be a tree. She could see its trunk and branches. But she had never before seen such a tree.

Where leaves would be in summer, there were clusters and streamers of thin green paper. Thick among them hung little sacks made of pink mosquito-bar. Laura was almost sure that she could see candy in them. From the branches hung packages wrapped in coloured paper, red packages and pink packages and yellow packages, all tied with coloured string. Silk scarves were draped among them. Red mittens hung by the cord that would go around your neck and keep them from being lost if you were wearing them. A pair of new shoes hung by their heels from a branch. Lavish strings of white popcorn were looped over all this.

Under the tree and leaning against it were all kinds of things. Laura saw a crinkly-bright washboard, a wooden tub, a churn and dasher, a sled made of new boards, a shovel, a long-handled pitchfork.

Laura was too excited to speak. She squeezed Mary's hand tighter and tighter, and she looked up at Ma, wanting so much to know what that was. Ma smiled down at her and answered, "That is a Christmas tree, girls. Do you think it is pretty?"

They could not answer. They nodded while they kept on looking at that wonderful tree. Just then Laura saw the most wonderful thing of all. From a far branch of that tree hung a little fur cape, and a muff to match!

The Reverend Alden was there. He preached about Christmas, but Laura was looking at that tree and she could not hear what he said. Everyone stood up to sing and Laura stood up, but she could not sing. Not a sound would come out of her throat. In the whole world, there couldn't be a store so wonderful to look at as that tree.

After the singing, Mr. Tower and Mr. Beadle began taking things off it, and reading out names. Everything on that tree was a Christmas present for somebody!

When Laura knew that, the lamps and people and voices and even the tree began to whirl. They whirled faster, noisier, and more excited. Someone gave her a pink mosquito-bar bag. It did have candy in it, and a big popcorn ball. Mary had one, too. So did Carrie. Every girl and boy had one. Then Mary had a pair of blue mittens. Then Laura had a red pair.

Ma opened a big package, and there was a warm, big, brown-and-red plaid shawl for her. Pa got a woolly muffler. Then Carrie had a rag doll with a china head. She screamed for joy. Through the laughing and talking and rustling of papers Mr. Beadle and Mr. Tower went on shouting names.

The little fur cape and muff still hung on the tree, and Laura wanted them. She wanted to look at them as long as she could. She wanted to know who got them. They could not be for Nellie Oleson who already had a fur cape.

Mr. Tower was taking the little fur cape and the muff from the tree. He read a name, but Laura could not hear it through all the joyful noise. She lost sight of the cape and muff among all the people. They were gone now.

There had never been such a Christmas as this. It was such a large, rich Christmas, the whole church full of Christmas. There were so many lamps, so many people, so much noise and laughter, and so many happinesses in it. Laura felt full and bursting, as if that whole big rich Christmas were inside her. And suddenly some- one said, "These are for you, Laura."

Mrs. Tower stood smiling, holding out the little fur cape and muff.

"For me?" Laura said. "For me?" Then everything else van- ished while with both arms she hugged the soft furs to her.

She hugged them tighter and tighter, trying to believe they were really hers, that silky-soft little brown fur cape and the muff.

All around her Christmas went on, but Laura knew only the softness of those furs. People were going home. Carrie was stand- ing on the bench while Ma fastened her coat and tied her hood more snugly. Ma was saying, "Thank you so much for the shawl, Brother Alden. It is just what I needed."

Pa said, "And I thank you for the muffler. It will feel good when I come to town in the cold."

The Reverend Alden sat down on the bench and asked, "And does Mary's coat fit?"

Laura had not noticed Mary's coat until then. Mary had on a new dark-blue coat. It was long, and its sleeves came down to Mary's wrists. Mary buttoned it up, and it fitted.

"And how does this little girl like her furs?" the Reverend Alden smiled. He drew Laura between his knees. He laid the fur cape around her shoulders and fastened it at the throat. He put the cord of the muff around her neck, and her hands went inside the silky muff.

"She's a little brown bird with red trimmings," the Reverend Alden said.

Then Laura laughed. It was true. Her hair and her coat, her

dress and the wonderful furs, were brown. Her hood and mittens and the braid on her dress were red.

"I'll tell my church people back East about our little brown bird," said the Reverend Alden. "You see, when I told them about our church out here, they said they must send a box for the Christmas tree. They all gave things they had. The little girls who sent your furs and Mary's coat needed larger ones."

"Thank you, sir," said Laura. "And please, sir, tell them thank you, too." For when she could speak, her manners were as nice as Mary's.

Then they all said good night and Merry Christmas to the Reverend Alden. Mary was so beautiful in her Christmas coat. Carrie was so pretty on Pa's arm. Pa and Ma were smiling so happily, and Laura was all gladness.

Mr. and Mrs. Oleson were going home, too. Mr. Oleson's arms were full of things, and so were Nellie's and Willie's. No wickedness boiled up in Laura now; she only felt a little bit of mean gladness.

"Merry Christmas, Nellie," Laura said. Nellie stared, while Laura walked quietly on, with her hands snuggled deep in the soft muff. Her cape was prettier than Nellie's, and Nellie had no muff.

NOW CHRISTMAS IS COME

Washington Irving

Now Christmas is come
    Let's beat up the drum,
And call all our neighbors together,
    And when they appear,
Let's make them such cheer
    As will keep out the wind and the
        weather.

little tree
e. e. cummings

little tree
little silent Christmas tree
you are so little
you are more like a flower

who found you in the green forest
and were you very sorry to come away?
see   i will comfort you
because you smell so sweetly

i will kiss your cool bark
and hug you safe and tight
just as your mother would,
only don't be afraid

look   the spangles
that sleep all the year in a dark box

dreaming of being taken out and allowed to shine,
the balls the chains red and gold the fluffy threads,

put up your little arms
and i'll give them all to you to hold
every finger shall have its ring
and there won't be a single place dark or unhappy

that when you're quite dressed
you'll stand in the window for everyone to see
and how they'll stare!
oh but you'll be very proud

and my little sister and i will take hands
and looking up at our beautiful tree
we'll dance and sing
"Noel Noel"

GO TELL IT ON THE MOUNTAIN
Traditional Spiritual

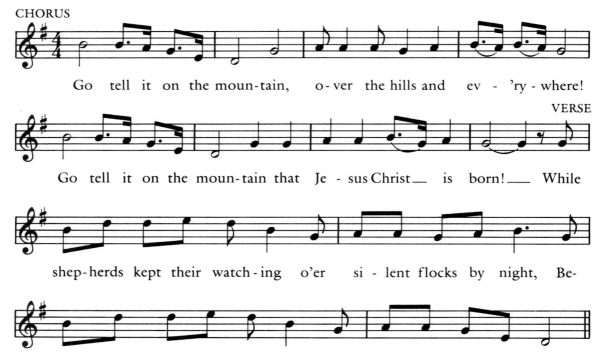

CHORUS

Go tell it on the moun-tain, o-ver the hills and ev-'ry-where!

VERSE

Go tell it on the moun-tain that Je-sus Christ___ is born!___ While

shep-herds kept their watch-ing o'er si-lent flocks by night, Be-

hold, through-out the heav-ens, there shone a ho-ly light.

CHORUS

Go tell it on the moun-tain, o-ver the hills and ev-'ry-where!

Go tell it on the moun-tain that Je-sus Christ— is born!

After each of the following verses, repeat the chorus.

The shepherds feared and trembled
When lo! above the earth
Rang out the angel chorus
That hailed our Jesus' birth.

Down in a lonely manger
The humble Christ was born,
And God sent out salvation
That blessed Christmas morn.

BRER RABBIT'S CHRISTMAS

Traditional American Tale

One winter morning, when he knew Brer Rabbit wasn't home, Brer Fox stole into Brer Rabbit's garden. He helped himself to every last one of Brer Rabbit's carrots and left with his bag so full it was bursting at the seams.

When Brer Rabbit got home and saw his garden with nothing much left to admire, he was mighty angry. He sped off directly to Brer Fox's house. The door was bolted and the shutters were closed tight. Brer Rabbit couldn't hear anything except the sound of his own stomach grumbling. But all around was the sweet smell of soup cooking.

Brer Rabbit knocked on the door. Bam Bam Bam. No answer.

"I know you're there, Brer Fox," called Brer Rabbit. "Now you open this door." No answer.

He knocked harder. Bam Bamity Bam. "I know those are my carrots in your soup," said Brer Rabbit, "and I want them back. Now open this door!"

Finally there was an answer from inside. "Too bad," said Brer Fox. "I ain't opening this door. I'm making enough soup in here to keep me till spring comes."

Brer Rabbit tried knocking the door in. He kicked at it and hammered on it, but that door didn't budge. Finally he gave up. He was hopping mad. Now you know that Brer Rabbit was the best at trickety tricking, and when he was mad, watch out.

But he could never stay mad long. And the next thing you know Brer Rabbit was chuckling. It hadn't taken him long to think of a plan to get his carrots back and make Brer Fox mad too.

On Christmas Eve, Brer Rabbit heaved a sackful of stones on his shoulder and climbed up on Brer Fox's roof. He clattered around making plenty of noise.

"Who's that up there?" called Brer Fox.

"It's Santa Claus," said Brer Rabbit in a gruff voice he hoped sounded like Santa Claus. "And I got a sackful of presents for you."

"Oh, you got presents for me?" said Brer Fox. "Well, you're most welcome here, Santa Claus. But ain't you supposed to come down the chimney?"

"Sure am," said Brer Rabbit in his Santa Claus voice. "But I can't. I'm stuck in the chimney. You want to see?"

Brer Fox unbolted the door and peered outside. "Well, don't come down then," he hollered up at the roof. "Just drop the presents down the chimney and I'll catch them."

"Can't," answered Brer Rabbit. "The sack is stuck too. But if you do what I say, I'd be mighty grateful. Climb up into the chimney. Then catch hold of this piece of string and pull the sack down yourself."

Brer Fox was only too happy to help. "That's easy," he said. "Here I come up the chimney."

He started clawing and scrabbling his way up.

Like lightning, Brer Rabbit leaped off that roof and into the doorway. There were his carrots in a pile, and on the stove was a big old pot of soup, all fragrant and bubbling, and on the table were some biscuits and mince pie, and there in the middle was the biggest, fattest Christmas pudding he'd ever seen. Brer Rabbit's mouth began to water at the sight of all that food. But he didn't waste much time. He grabbed as much as he could, stuffed it into his sack and took off running.

Meantime, Brer Fox was struggling to get up the chimney. He couldn't see any string, but he felt it hanging down. So he gave a pull. The sack opened and out tumbled all the stones right on Brer Fox's head. My goodness, he went down that chimney fast.

That rascally Brer Rabbit laughed at how he'd taken care of Brer Fox. But he kept out of Brer Fox's way all that Christmas day and for some time afterward.

MERRY CHRISTMAS
Aileen Fisher

I saw on the snow
when I tried my skis
the track of a mouse
beside some trees.

Before he tunneled
to reach his house
he wrote "Merry Christmas"
in white, in mouse.

CHRISTMAS EVE RHYME

Carson McCullers

My best friend is Jimmy
He has no chimney.
So what will happen at Christmas time?
When Santa flies over the houses
And stops at each chimney
Will he skip Jimmy
Who has no chimney?

SILVER BELLS

Jay Livingston and Ray Evans

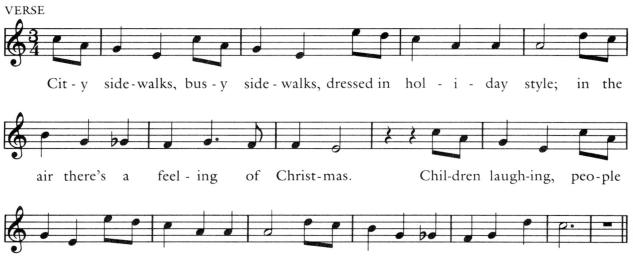

VERSE

Cit - y side-walks, bus - y side - walks, dressed in hol - i - day style; in the
air there's a feel - ing of Christ-mas. Chil-dren laugh-ing, peo-ple
pass-ing, meet-ing smile af - ter smile; and on ev - 'ry street cor-ner you'll hear:

CHORUS

Sil - ver bells,   sil - ver bells,   it's Christ-mas time in the cit - y.

Ring - a - ling,   hear them ring,   soon it will be Christ-mas day._____

After the following verse, repeat the chorus.

Strings of streetlights, even stoplights,
Blink a bright red and green,
As the shoppers rush home with their treasures.
Hear the snow crunch, see the kids bunch,
This is Santa's big scene,
And above all this bustle you hear:

THE NIGHT
BEFORE CHRISTMAS
Thyra Turner

Charity Moore stood at a large oak table in the great kitchen in Chelsea House. There was an unusual rush of work because tomorrow would be Christmas and guests were expected soon.

"Father said if we were very good, he would write a special poem for us for Christmas," said Charity.

"Your father's a very busy man," replied Susan the cook. "I'd hardly think he'd have time for poems for anybody."

Old Peter came into the kitchen with his arms full of evergreen boughs he had gathered from the woodlands near Hudson's River. He had taken care of the gardens at Chelsea for many years. Peter had a beautiful flowing white beard and his face was red and ruddy. His blue eyes twinkled merrily and when he laughed, as he often did, there were dimples in his cheeks.

Christmas was a busy time for old Peter. Fires had to be started in the fireplaces in the rooms where the guests were to sleep and more logs had to be carried to each room.

At that moment Dr. Moore came into the kitchen too. "Peter," he said, "I must travel to New York. Please hitch up the sleigh and put in plenty of robes. I believe there will be more snow before I return."

Peter was off and in a very short time the sleigh was at the door, the sleighbells jingling each time the horse moved or tossed her head. Peter held the reins while Dr. Moore got in and wrapped the warm robes about his body and legs.

The sleigh crunched over the hard white snow, past the few houses that dotted the fields about Chelsea. On and on they went through the Greenwich Village, far down the Broad Way.

"I will not be long, Peter," said Dr. Moore, as they drew up before a small white house, "I'll just leave this package and be out directly. Then I have a few purchases to make."

It was a pleasant trip and before long they were homeward bound, the sleigh piled high with gifts.

It had been cloudy all day but as the sun went down beyond the Hudson, the sky cleared, and a bright moon was rising as the sleigh again reached the village of Greenwich.

Then Dr. Moore thought of the poem that he had promised to write for the children. "A Christmas poem," he mused, "the Christ Child, the shepherds, the star, St. Nicholas. Yes, of course, St. Nicholas. But what did St. Nicholas look like?"

Just then Peter turned his head. His white beard glistened in the moonlight. Dr. Moore leaned forward and looked more closely at Peter. "The very man for the piece," he said to himself, "a typical St. Nicholas. Here I am with a sleigh full of toys and St. Nicholas too, on the night before Christmas!"

Suddenly the words of the poem seemed to be tumbling about him in the air.

When they reached Chelsea House he went upstairs to his desk and sat there for some time, covering many pages of paper with his fine handwriting.

At last the verses were finished and he found his family and friends in the drawing room before the fireplace.

Little Clement gave a great shout of welcome as his father entered the room. Charity ran and took his hand. "Did you write it?" she whispered as Dr. Moore took his seat.

"Yes," he whispered.

So while the family and guests sat about the blazing Christmas fire, Dr. Moore began to read his poem, *A Visit from St. Nicholas.*

'Twas the night before Christmas, when all through the house
Not a creature was stirring, not even a mouse;
The stockings were hung by the chimney with care,
In hopes that St. Nicholas soon would be there;
The children were nestled all snug in their beds,
While visions of sugar-plums danced in their heads;
And Mama in her 'kerchief, and I in my cap,
Had just settled our brains for a long winter's nap;
When out on the lawn there arose such a clatter,
I sprang from the bed to see what was the matter.

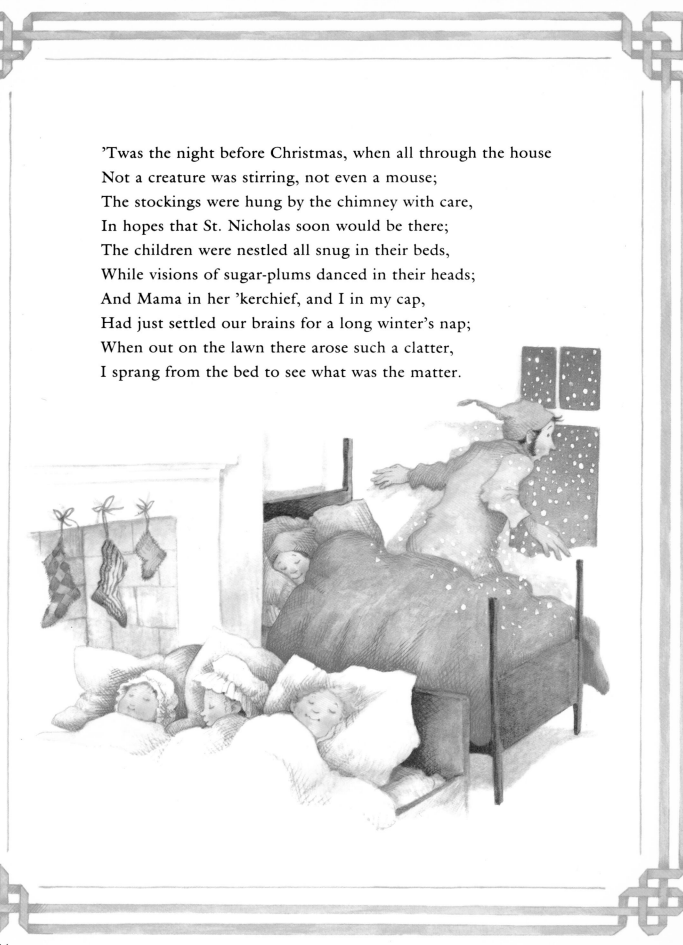

Away to the window I flew like a flash,

Tore open the shutters and threw up the sash.

The moon, on the breast of the new fallen snow,

Gave the lustre of mid-day to objects below

When, what to my wondering eyes should appear,

But a miniature sleigh, and eight tiny reindeer,

With a little old driver, so lively and quick,

I knew in a moment it must be St. Nick.

More rapid than eagles his coursers they came,

And he whistled, and shouted, and called them by name:

"Now, Dasher! now, Dancer! now, Prancer, and Vixen!

On, Comet! on, Cupid! on, Donder and Blitzen!

To the top of the porch! to the top of the wall!

Now dash away! dash away! dash away, all!"

As dry leaves that before the wild hurricane fly,

When they meet with an obstacle, mount to the sky;

So up to the housetop the coursers they flew,

With the sleigh full of toys, and St. Nicholas too.

And then, in a twinkling, I heard on the roof
The prancing and pawing of each little hoof—
As I drew in my head, and was turning around,
Down the chimney St. Nicholas came with a bound.
He was dressed all in fur, from his head to his foot,
And his clothes were all tarnished with ashes and soot;
A bundle of toys he had flung on his back,
And he look'd like a pedlar just opening his pack.
His eyes—how they twinkled! his dimples how merry!
His cheeks were like roses, his nose like a cherry!
His droll little mouth was drawn up like a bow,
And the beard on his chin was as white as the snow;
The stump of a pipe he held tight in his teeth,
And the smoke it encircled his head like a wreath;

He had a broad face and a little round belly
That shook, when he laughed, like a bowl full of jelly.
He was chubby and plump, a right jolly old elf,
And I laughed when I saw him in spite of myself.
A wink of his eye and a twist of his head
Soon gave me to know I had nothing to dread;
He spoke not a word, but went straight to his work,
And fill'd all the stockings; then turned with a jerk,
And laying his finger aside of his nose,
And giving a nod, up the chimney he rose.

He sprang to his sleigh, to his team gave a whistle,
And away they all flew like the down of a thistle.
But I heard him exclaim, ere he drove out of sight,
"Happy Christmas to all, and to all a good night."

There was a round of applause as Dr. Moore finished reading.

"I think it is the nicest poem you have ever written for us, Father," said Charity, "and I shall learn it by heart."

At this moment Susan entered the room with trays heaped high with sandwiches and cookies. Old Peter brought in mugs of hot cider and they all drank a toast to "the poet of Chelsea."

The fire burned and crackled. The old clock in the hall chimed the hour. It was getting late and almost time for St. Nicholas to come and fill the stockings.

Charity took little Clement's hand and when they were halfway up the long staircase she leaned far over the balustrade and throwing a kiss to her father and his guests below, she called "Happy Christmas to all, and to all a good night!"